DOGGIE
DAY OUT!

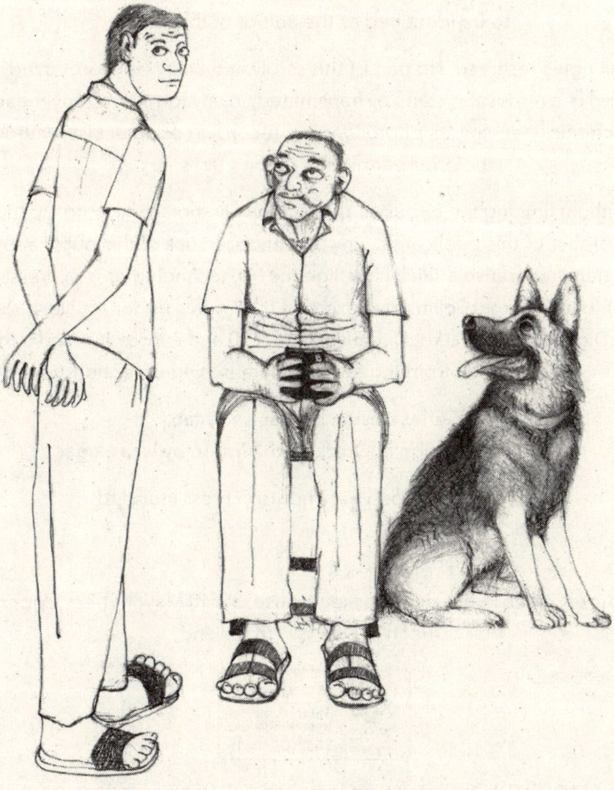

First published in India by HarperCollins *Children's Books* 2025
An imprint of HarperCollins *Publishers*

HarperCollins Publishers India, Cyber City, Building 10-A,
Gurugram, Haryana-122002, India

www.harpercollins.co.in

2 4 6 8 10 9 7 5 3 1

Text © Cyrus Broacha 2025
Illustrations © HarperCollins *Publishers* India 2025

P-ISBN: 978-93-6989-174-0
E-ISBN: 978-93-6989-347-8

Cyrus Broacha asserts the moral right
to be identified as the author of this work.

All rights reserved. No part of this publication may be reproduced, stored in a retrieval system, or transmitted, in any form or by any means, electronic, mechanical, photocopying, recording or otherwise, without the prior permission of the publishers.

Without limiting the exclusive rights of any author, contributor or the publisher of this publication, any unauthorized use of this publication to train generative artificial intelligence (AI) technologies is expressly prohibited. HarperCollins also exercise their rights under Article 4(3) of the Digital Single Market Directive 2019/790 and expressly reserve this publication from the text and data-mining exception.

Series design by Denise Antao
Layout and design in Quicksand 10pt/16 by Isha Nagar

Printed and bound at Thomson Press India Ltd

*

HarperCollins Publishers, Macken House, 39/40 Mayor Street Upper,
Dublin 1, D01 C9W8, Ireland

This book is produced from independently certified FSC® paper
to ensure responsible forest management.

DOGGIE
DAY OUT!

CYRUS BROACHA

ILLUSTRATED BY
AYESHA BROACHA

HARPERCOLLINS
CHILDREN'S BOOKS

This, for lack of a better word,
book is dedicated to all the animal haters
of India. The ones who stop us feeding, pull their
kids away from animals, throw stones unnecessarily
at dogs and cats, and are generally filled with
negative energy.

This book is for you with a pleasant message
attached. Migrate. Please, feel free
to migrate. Thanks in advance. Also, have to
dedicate this 'thing' to all the beautiful souls that
stayed with me from childhood. To Figaro, Don
Giovanni, Luciano, Volpi, Ruffo, Peter and Mary ...
till we meet again.

PROLOGUE

This was never supposed to be a book. It was supposed to be just a few words, scribbled on the wall that a dog with any sense would have peed on. Then it evolved into a leaflet. Soon it became a chapter, and then, like the acorn occasionally becomes a tree (which a dog with any sense will pee on), the chapter then rolled into a full book.

For me, it is a great honour to be the chosen one. Chosen by 'Franco' the author, who also happens to be a doggie, to write the introduction to this, his seventh book. The first six have all done swimmingly well, with 'Dog Day Afternoon and Morning' winning the prestigious 'Golden Paw' award in Oslo, Norway. Franco's last book, 'Communicating thru Potty', is in line for this year's Bowker. Last month it swept the 'BARK' awards, where along with Best Novelist, Franco won an award for the 'Longest Paragraph'— a paragraph so long that it has not yet been completed! First though, a word about Franco. Franco is a five- year-old German Shepherd dog, although, he prefers the word 'Alsatian'. This is because, Franco, as can be seen from his name, is a huge Francophile. Franco lives in a house opposite to me, and we've enjoyed a fabulous relationship these last five years or so. I don't want to toot my own horn, sorry, praise my own woof, but it was I who persuaded Franco into becoming a writer. I could see his potential from a very early incident.

This happened when Franco was still only a little puppy. It was his first car ride with the window open. Franco was having a whale of a time. A passerby who came close to the window, *may* have, I repeat, may have had his shirt sleeve ripped off. However, with no CCTV footage, or independent witness accounts, this act could not be confirmed. There was no solid proof to pin this crime solely on Franco. When Franco's human mother asked if he had indeed done this deed of violence, Franco spun a fabulous tale. 'Mom it was my first car ride. I was super excited taking in all the new sights and sounds, though of course, not smells. You know there are no nice smells left in the city of Mumbai; for that we will have to go to Nashik, I believe. So, yes, I did have my mouth open, when the passerby passed our barely moving car, and I opened it wider, not to bite his sleeve, but in amazement as I saw a kite swoop down on the guy and, in one clean swoop, peel off his sleeve. After this it flew away in the evening sky. I barked at the perplexed passerby to explain what had happened. But since he did not speak, Dogolease, he presumed I was attacking him, since his shirt had just been torn off. Tell me if humans can be so slow, so stupid and so un-preceptive, how did they ever become the most advanced in the animal kingdom? No come on, tell me? You say? I'm waiting. Tell me, explain? No answer? What's going on?'

Franco was so good at inventing stories like this, that his mom felt guilty about the accusations and bought Franco a whole family tub of vanilla ice-cream as compensation. (Sorry, my publisher says we can't mention brands.)

As for the passerby, who had been chased away by the building watchman, forget ice-cream, he lost his sleeve, he lost his dignity and he lost his mind. Poor guy. But what to do, nobody can challenge the legendary Alsatian. Now over to Franco.

Hi, this is Franco, your friendly neighbourhood Alsatian. This is my story, so obviously the views and opinions are all mine. Take them with a pinch of salt (or not). Most importantly, enjoy the story!

CHAPTER 1

Call me, Franco.

Okay sorry about that, it's just that I'm a huge Moby Dick fan. Yes, yes, dogs can read. I mean it's common knowledge. Do I have to unteach everything your school teaches you? For Dog's sake! Fine Hoomans, let's start again. Hello to you all, I'm the author of this book, and I'm recounting a tale of great suspense and intrigue. Oh, and every word of this book is absolutely true. Well, almost every word. Well, honestly, about half of the book. I guess, if push comes to shove, about 30% would be marked authentic. To be fair, I've just been informed by the publisher that we can't verify even a single word in this book as scrupulously true. So please ignore this last paragraph and keep in mind during this journey, I will constantly remind you to ignore many other such paragraphs. True or not, we can't go forward with this tale of One City, without giving you what Gen Z calls a 'background'.

I'm a five-year-old Alsatian. I'm extremely well read and well informed. For those who don't know much about Alsatians, here goes. We are not the fastest dog, or the strongest, or the most agile, or the most intelligent. However, we are the second best at everything. Hence, we are similar to top all-rounders in cricket. (Just using references you Hoomans can relate to.) In other words, we are similar to great all-rounders like Hardik Pandya or Ben Stokes.

Back to the background. I live with my adopted family, the Treasurywallas. Thus, my full name as listed on my Aadhaar card is Franco Faredoon Treasurywalla. I have been with this family since I was eight weeks old, and I'll come to them in a minute. When I first arrived, I was a little anxious as the area, Malabar Hill, had a new fad going on called 'vegetarianism'. I didn't want to land up in a vegetarian setting as I love my food very much. Luckily, the Treasurywallas love their meat, so much, that they constantly threaten to eat me. No, seriously, they keep saying things like, 'Franco, you are so yummy, I want to eat you up'. Initially, I was so confused by these remarks that I avoided walking into the kitchen just in case I didn't get to walk out.

The building where we live is an eight-storey one, built in 1962. I know all this because I am a great fan of architecture. I've always been fascinated with shapes and designs. I give a huge amount of study time to a building's façade, interiors, aesthetic feel, and solidity, before I pee on it. Colour combinations, sunlight position as well as surrounding buildings and structures, are all very fascinating to me. I unfriended my oldest friend Natasha, a Dalmatian, because she once told me, 'A building is just a building, and all buildings look the same'. I replied with 'A Dalmatian is just a Dalmatian, and all Dalmatians look the same'. Still, she didn't have to bite my tail. Twice!!

Our residence, is on the fourth floor of a building called 'Aras'. Yes, the word Aras makes no sense. But here's the scoop behind it. Aras was owned and built in the 60s by the Kharas family. On final completion, the painter painting the building's name at the front ran out of paint. He had just about enough for four letters written in capitals. Old man Cawas Kharas was an incredibly impatient man. He compromised to save time, and settled for an incomplete spelling of the family name. That is how 'Kharas' became 'Aras'. Oh, and thanks to the Mumbai monsoon, it should soon evolve (or dissolve) to 'Ras'.

Now that I've broken convention and started in the middle, let me go back to the beginning. Oh, and just to keep you Hoomans on your toes, I may jump from the middle to the beginning, or to the end and back again. This may confuse Hoomans, but my dog readers will understand and appreciate that we dogs aren't limited to linear, chronological thinking patterns. That's the occupational hazard of being Hooman. Canids can, and always will think out of the box, up and down, crisscrossing the dimensions of time. Oops, my paw is paining, let me change paws. Yes, we dogs are all ambidextrous. Oh, and by that, I mean, not just right paw and left paw; the fact is we can write with all four paws. And someone said Hoomans are the advanced species? Such humour is not appreciated, thank you!

Let's go back then. As I was saying, I entered the Aras building roughly five years ago, and though memory is scant, I can piece together a few of them. Now, before you complain and whine, keep in mind five weeks for an Alsatian is like a eight months for Hooman baby. Kindly write down all your memories of when you were four months, and hand it to me. Let's start with my Hooman mom.

Her name was, and is, Pereena, though everybody calls her Perry. In fact, you Hoomans have this bad habit of finding things funny even though they make no sense. Pereena's pet name was 'Dirty Perry'. Apparently, this was given to her as a twelve-year-old, as she was the first girl in her class to use foul language. Words, my publisher says, I can't reproduce here because our readership starts at the age of six months. Perry also had a catch phrase that she repeatedly employed. Luckily, it's a non-controversial phrase, so I can produce it here. She often says in a

quizzical tone, 'Em che', this roughly translates from the Parsee Gujarati into 'Is that so'. Sometimes, she adds an expletive after 'Em che', but I can't reproduce them, as I said before, so stop bugging me and write directly to the publisher whose name I forget as my last meal was two whole hours ago.

Dirty Perry is the first face I remember. She's the one who taught me how to count. You may not believe this, but the first Hooman number that I learnt was thirty-seven. And I was forced to learn it. In fact, it's quite a dirty story. And by dirty, I mean unhygienic. That's because Dirty Perry picked me up and kissed me thirty-seven times the first time she saw me. I kept a count of every kiss. Halfway through, I swear I couldn't breathe; by the thirty-seventh kiss, I was on life support. Please Hoomans, I'm a GSD. Two or three kisses are enough, then please throw the ball. If you want to kiss thirty-seven times, get a Shih Tzu, for God's sake, sorry, make that Dog's sake. Dirty Perry is what we dogs like to call an 'OKH'. OKH stands for Over Kissing Hoomans. I request each one of you to find your family OKH. Then have a stern word. Kisses must have a limit. Love, just like hate, can be overdosed for Dog's sake! By the way, Dirty Perry is pretty pretty. Okay, I confused you? Dirty Perry is nice looking. Why do I bring this up? Well, we GSDs are very good looking. No arrogance here, just stating facts. Nothing hurts the eye more than a good-looking GSD in a family of Ughs. By Ughs, I mean unattractive Hoomans. This gets compounded if one of the Ughs is an OKH. Rule of Paw is:

Good Looking Canine, Good Looking Family. Actually, now I feel a real sense of responsibility in writing this book. You see, while writing, I am simultaneously realizing that I have to educate Hoomans, who claim to know so much about dogs but actually have no clue. Maybe we'll change the tittle to 'The Dogwalker's Guide to the Universe'.

The next Treasurywalla is Perry's hubby, Homi. Now, that's my kind of Hooman. Homi is what we dogs call a mixed bag. Not to say he is a bag, or bag-like in any way, shape or capacity. It's just that he is tall, well built, good looking (for a Hooman. Hoomans, as you know, are not a very physically attractive species, no judgement here), but he has a very thin voice. The voice is soft and at odds with his appearance. Imagine a big tall burly Cane Corso with the voice of a Pekinese. Yet, Homi is the nicest guy in the world. He always puts me first, like a good father should. He doesn't make a great song and dance of his love, but he always plans my days—my walks, my food, my toys, which books I read, that kind of thing.

Right from my first day, Homi had one rule. He didn't want any outsiders being walked by me. 'Franco must be walked by the family alone.' (Homi mixes up his words often. He meant to say 'The family must be walked by Franco alone'.) He felt that there was a sacred contract in place between family and dog. This contract must be honoured at all costs. He made a table out and put it on the fridge. It said, 'Dog Waking Table for Franco' (what it actually meant to say was 'Hooman Walking Table for Franco' because I'm the one who takes them on walks for the sake of their health. Hoomans are really bad at grammar). 6.00am Homi, 10.00am Homi, 2.00pm Homi, 6.00pm Homi, and 10.00pm Homi. (If Homi unavailable, then any other family member. If no family member available, then any blood relative.) As a consequence of this, Homi looked down on other dog people. Okay, I lied. He didn't look down; he despised them. Again, this publisher is restraining me from printing the filthy language he would use to describe them. Then that Dirty Perry would join the chanting, and it would sound almost as bad as techno music to this dog's discerning ears. Yet, Homi made me feel like a million bucks. Make that 10 million bucks. He treated me like a diamond to be cared for and watched over twenty-four hours a day, seven days a week. All his friends would say the same thing to him. When we pass, we want to come back reincarnated as your dog. Dirty Perry was actually worried that she'd be pushed off the bed in order to accommodate me. Let me be clear here: I am on the bed, all three of us are . . . er, as of now.

That brings us to another doggie-Hooman classification: Hoomans with doggies on the bed vs those who expect doggies to sleep in their own separate tiny beds. My friend Simba, the Labrador, (yes, yes, I know there are forty-three Labradors called Simba, in our neighbourhood. This is No. 29) is not allowed on the Hoomans' bed. So, when he comes over, he virtually stays for the entire duration on my

bed. Homi and Dirty Perry love this. Like I said, two types of Hoomans. One like the Treasurywallas, and other a bunch of uneducated simpletons who think dogs should be just dogs. Imagine the cheek! Dogs should be just dogs???

Next in our family is Roxan. No, Roxaaan. Forget it, spellings are tough. I call her Roxy. At the time of my Hooman birth, Roxy was a young girl with braces. Now, a few years on, she's a teenage girl with braces. Roxy's critical flaw? She's a hugger. Just like her mom, who is a kisser, this one's an absolute hugger. What's with you Hoomans? Can't you tell a GSD's coat is his fortune, his badge of honour? Like Beyoncé's voice. Or Neeraj Chopra's arm. You don't mess with a GSD's coat, unless you want to lose your fingers. Oh, and by the way, I do prefer Alsatian, but my publisher has asked me to stick to GSD.

Roxy, I find very noisy. Sweet, but noisy, and she must cut back on the hugging. I mean, I'm a seventy-pound canine. I shudder to think what would happen to a ten-pound Shih Tzu? Wouldn't last a week. But before you think I'm some heartless GSD, Roxy's got a great habit that makes her one of my favourite Hoomans. She feeds me under the table. I don't mean a bribe. I mean, she's one of those picky eaters. You know every family has them. Not only is she picky, she's also awfully slow at eating. Breakfast averages forty-five minutes. And that's just one egg! So, as a solution, to help her eat, I volunteer to carry that load for her. Every meal we follow the 80/20 rule famous in the world of nutrition: I eat 80%, she 20%. This is, in my opinion, why dogs are truly man's best friend. We are always there when you need us most. Like breakfast, lunch and dinner.

Yup, that's the four of us Treasurywallas. Now sit back as I start my tale of suspense, intrigue, and .... I've left space for you to add your own adjective.

CHAPTER 2

It all started last June. No, was it July, August? I'm not too sure. Stop with the pressure. All I know is it all started a while back. I got the news while I was outside the disfigured Parag Building, which I often use as my personal toilet. Yup, I was peeing when they told me what happened. It was basically a kidnapping.

Before I proceed, let me make it clear, I'm not a racist. Let's correct that, I'm not a complete dogist. But do consider, we dogs do discriminate on the grounds of breed, height, gender, double coat, weight, barking ability and many more categories. In the CCA (Canine Character Almanac), these differences are encouraged, and for one dog to be disparaging to another dog is not a crime in the least. For a Great Dane to tell a Dachshund to 'Buzz off, Shortybhai', is par for the course. The difference between canines and

Hoomans in this regard is dogs are open and immediate in their dogism and prejudices.

Now, here's the sequence of events. I had reached my personal public urinal at Parag Building, where I also walk Homi most mornings and evenings. After considering seventeen different scents, I had marked my spot, raised my left hind leg and was just about to unleash a spray on an unsuspecting stone, when the Parag Building watchman informed Homi that there had been a kidnapping. Homi and I, of course, were least interested; that is, till he clarified it was a dog and not a Hooman that had been kidnapped.

Dognapping, now that's a different story. So shocked was I, that I stopped mid-pee. Which, as you all know, is a horrible feeling. But Homi was worse off—his ruddy face became crimson with anger and he started choking the poor helpless watchman to glean more information. I tugged on the leash to restrain Homi. Dog knows all that leash training seems wasted on Hoomans. When the watchman regained his composure, this is what he said. I translate indiscriminately, because I've never really been good at picking up the accents of non-Treasurywallas, but here goes. 'Saab, Mrs Subramanian's expensive dog Hakuna Matata was kidnapped two hours ago while on his walk with the house help Prasad. The dog is an expensive breed called an "Offo Panchee".' As Homi nodded gravely, there were three things I picked up immediately:

1. The watchman had no respect for or interest in Mr Subramanian.

2. The dog was already suffering as he was named after a phrase. A full phrase was his actual name!

3. The watchman had less than zero knowledge about exotic dog breeds. Offo Panchee sounded more like someone screaming in pain in Bengali. It certainly wasn't one of the 224 registered dog breeds. Nor the few hundred indigenous ones of our country.

Homi and I wasted no time. The distance to the Subramanians, who lived two buildings away, was covered in less than half a minute. Mrs Lalita Subramanian was inconsolable. The kajal from her eyes had entered her mouth space, and it looked like she had her COVID mask on. Knowing his twisted sense of humour, I decided to cut Homi short before he started, reminding him this was no time for jokes. Within minutes, delayed by some copious sobbing from Mrs Subramanian as she tried to explain, we had figured out a few important facts about this case:

Fact 1. The dog was not 'Offo Panchee'. In fact, he was an 'Affenpinscher'.

Fact 2. Since he was a full-grown dog but weighed 8 pounds, was it worth getting him back? I mean, 8 pounds!

Fact 3. For some absurd reason despite Mr. Subramanian being a double MBA PhD, the couple paid 2 lacs for this, er ... 8 pounds. Just shows you, wisdom can't be taught, and education is so overrated. (Phew.)

Fact 4. Hakuna Matata was the name chosen by their astrologer, who insisted the name would be lucky for the dog. Of course, there was this small matter of the astrologer's son starring in his school adaptation of 'The Lion King'.

Homi, without consulting me, assured Mrs Subramanian that we'd find Hakuna Matata. Then he went and added, 'Dead or alive'. I've never seen a Hooman cry so much as Mrs. Subramanian did on hearing his words. I pulled on Homi's leash; our work at the Subramanians was done. Homi and I rushed home and shared the news with Dirty Perry and Roxy. Everyone was aghast, stunned. I mean, who names their dog Hakuna Matata? I quickly pulled out my Dogcyclopedia Bhowtannica. I'd never heard of an Affenpinscher and, since I was the dog, the Treasurywallas were looking to my expertise and leadership in the matter.

Now hold on bacchas and bacchees, let me introduce you to this dog, this Affenpinscher. It's a German name, meaning 'Monkey Dog'. Frankly, upon reading this, I already felt like letting Hakuna Matata go. I mean, it's one thing to rescue a fellow canine, but if we're unsure whether it's a monkey or a dog? I mean, that's another thing altogether. I've never liked monkeys, for crying out loud. They are like better-looking Hoomans with even worse manners.

Anyway, on the assumption that the Affenpinscher is indeed a canine, I'll go ahead. They are generally black in colour, weigh around 10 pounds, and make excellent watchdogs. At this point, I was hysterical with laughter. Let me set this up for you. An 8 to 10 pound thing, perhaps monkey, perhaps dog, with a name like Hakuna Matata makes for a great watchdog?! I was in serious doubt about the credibility of my Dogcyclopedia Bhowtannica. I quickly made the relevant correction, replacing the 'watchdog' with 'paper weight'. And, so began the case of the missing Monkey Dog Hakuna Matata, all of 8 pounds.

CHAPTER 3

The first thing to do was to lighten my load. That is, to get rid of Homi. Homi's great, a smashing Hooman. I'd say, he has fewer than seventeen bad habits. Now, that's a pretty good average for a Hooman. But he does this very annoying thing. He talks. Not just that, he talks when I'm thinking. Homi knows that I'm the brain in our partnership, yet he feels the need to do this irritating thing. So I took action.

I dropped Homi at Aras and made my first move. I scratched my left ear that always itches. I gave it a good scratch. Then I made my second move. I began the hunt for 'Raju'. 'Who Raju?, you ask? Well, let me tell you that in Urban India, 79% of Hoomans employ a person to accompany their dog on their sauntering. I have the data, (which I dare not share with you) that shows that 22% of the professional walkers return home with just the empty leash. These dog walkers are a bit of a paradox. Interestingly, most of these walkers are named 'Raju'. Don't ask me why. Unless you are reading this in Persian. I'm a dog not a god. I had no hand in creating Hooman kind. If I did, I'd have given them all tails.

What was not at all clear is where exactly Hakuna Matata was dognapped, and who the hell was with him at that time.

The watchman (one of the great Hooman detectives of this era) claimed that it was just outside the building and that 'Raju', disguised under the name Prasad, was with him when the crime actually occurred. Immediately, my mind was swamped with these questions:

(a) Was the watchman lying?

(b) Was Raju aka Prasad lying?

(c) Was Hakuna Matata lying?

Only one way to find out. I had to recreate the crime. The watchman had a peculiar smell. May I be candid? Brutally honest? Please don't mind, but all Hoomans stink. Sometimes, when there's a collection of Hoomans, it becomes unbearable to any self-respecting dog. If you catch one of us with our head down, desperately trying to smell the ground below us, it is because we are trying to get away from the rancid, almost acidic smell of Hoomanity. The very memory recall of all this is making me want to abandon writing this book. Yet, nasty as the smell may be, each Hooman has a unique stench, which is unreplicated by any other individual Hooman on the entire planet. Hence, instead of one bad aroma, we have billions and billions of horrible smells filtering through our über-developed doggie nostrils. And then, on top of that, you all have the cheek to put on perfumes and deodorants? Come on Hoomans, have mercy on us doggies, please!

Back to the watchman, I can't remember his name, so I'm calling him Smelly. However, since that may sound a little disrespectful, I'll call him Smellji. I needed to be patient. As we dogs like to say, 'Rome wasn't built in a day'. I have a date to show it was in fact a whole weekend. By the way, Rome was built by my ancestors Romulus and Remus, who were raised by wolves. Just a fun fact Hoomans may not be aware of.

Smellji was a low-movement Hooman. He sat on a stool and listened to songs on his phone all day long. I think the word 'watch' in watchman stands for 'watching' programmes on phones. But I couldn't stake out Smellji for too long. After an hour or so, Homi would start worrying and come looking for me. Twice before, when I've been on important security-related reconnaissance missions, he has sabotaged my work. I still remember Jacky, the neighbourhood mutt, whom I had tried getting some classified information regarding leftover bones out of, and then at the most crucial juncture, Homi appeared and said, 'Baba, where have you been, your food is getting cold'. Then, he had the temerity to whisk me off, letting Jacky go scot-free, dashing my hopes of finding where the bones were hidden. Keeping all these factors in mind, I positioned myself next to Smellji. I found a place where he'd never notice me, right next to his feet. The idea was to stay put, wait, observe and note down.

For fifty-seven minutes, nothing happened. Smellji just went on listening to his inane music, which is very hard on Hooman ears, but even worse on doggie ears. Finally, I got what I was waiting for. A man stopped by to talk to Smellji.

CHAPTER 4

Hoomans, it amazes me how you think. You guys keep saying that you are the most advanced species. Based on what? That some of you have learnt how to flush after going to the toilet? With all your so called 'scientific achievements', you guys still cannot do basic things. For instance, you can't clean your whole body using just your tongue. You wear clothes even on the hottest of days for some reason. And, and this is a huge and (which, by the way, is a new world record for using the word 'and' so many times in a sentence), Hoomans cannot tell if a person is good or bad just from their scent. Hoomans, I don't know which word applies more correctly to describe your species. Backward, primitive, or challenged. I suppose, it's best if we use all three. Let me clarify here. We canines and most mammals can pick up the scent of people which we can read like a book. Like this man who came to chat with Smellji, I picked up that he was vegetarian, was forty-four years old, suffered from asthma and hemorrhoids, had just eaten a paan, which he failed to digest, and was currently suffering from irritable bowel syndrome. Also, he was left-handed, and other less relevant information, such as his affinity for pav vada over vada pav, and that he always preferred his dosa crisp, but that is part of another story, so I won't share that with you here. (My publisher keeps shouting, 'Stick to relevance!' Such a repetitive species you are).

The man, as I overheard, was named Chandu. What immediately hit me from his scent was that he had bad energy. We doggies can tell bad energy from good energy immediately. There's a difference between bad energy and a bad Hooman. All Hoomans are capable of bad energy. Just watch them drive in traffic, and my point is proven. However, if the energy is bad for long periods of time, then it's not a bout of bad energy. Instead, it is clearly a bad person. Chandu kept looking sideways, wary of being seen for some reason. You know the pattern. A Hooman trying to look calm, works so hard at his calmness, that you can see him shivering. His main bone of contention was, had anyone seen the person who nicked 'Hakuna Matata'. Of course, he used the name 'Aku Batata', which is a phrase that rolls easier off a North Indian speaker's tongue?

Hold on, let me pick up on the clues.

Clue 1. Why does he care so much?

Clue 2. Why is he trying to act like he's not nervous, and thus coming off as super nervous?

Clue 3. How does he know if only one person kidnapped 'Hakuna Matata', oops, sorry, 'Aku Batata'? How could he know it was one male, and not many males, or a female, or many females, or males and females, or a female and males, or a male and females? You get my point.

Smellji, let's be frank, is not a gifted philosopher. In fact, he's what you call a lazy thinker. The ones who believe in economy of thought. As in, thinking weighs them down. Tires them out. Hence, good old Smellji doesn't like to have more than one thought a week. Obviously, such a person hates questions. Questions, go hand in hand with their partner, answers. Answers demand the use of thought. Also, questions demand the use of focusing and paying attention, which is ten times more tiring then even those thoughts. Basically, Smellji was happy to be a low intensity gossip, but when the questions increased, his interest decreased. His eyes got dull, his blood pressure dropped, his faculties started shutting down, (and yet, you are the so-called 'apex species'). Once the two got tired of each other, Chandu walked away. What he didn't know was that a large German Shepherd or, as I prefer, Alsatian, was following him.

The lane that runs just to the right of Aras has many buildings. Four of them look like they have decent living conditions. None of the four are above nine floors. They're all clean and painted regularly. The people living in them are called the 'Haves' by fellow Hoomans. The four buildings opposite the 'Haves' are decrepit, run down and basically look as old as the city itself. Chandu disappeared into one of these buildings, which was originally white in colour, but now consists of a mixture of four colours haphazardly arranged about it. A little grey, a little black and some sort of brown. The lower floor has every stain available. Daal stains, paan stains, parts of old chappatis which have turned into little rocks, plastic bottles strewn about and even some areas where the cement has expired. The building is called 'Sea View'. Here we see Hoomans at their very best. The sea is 4 kms away. Oh, and yes, it can't be seen from this building. It would be more appropriate to call this thing 'No Sea View'. Maybe the builder named it in the hope that one day the sea will come closer.

Sea view or no sea view, I lost my Chandu view. The building had a narrow entrance. I am, let's face it, ruggedly handsome. If I was a Hooman, I'd be John Abraham. Too conspicuous, I needed backup. Using a howl, I called up my street friend, Bhilla. Bhilla of course, is what we term a 'desi' doggie. He lives on the streets and is looked after by

a cobbler named Phoolan. Desi doggies are the toughest custards around. They survive everything. Always in danger from evil bikers, motorists, cruel pedestrians, the monsoon and firecrackers. Yet they have unbelievable resilience. Hoomans won't understand. You people are too soft. One pandemic and you hid at home for a year, hiding behind masks. Yet, Hoomans look down on rats. The mind boggles. How can the most advanced species have no concept of reality?

As soon as I howled, Bhilla appeared out of nowhere. Bhilla adores me. I mean, when I was a pup, he did try the domination game, but as I explained to him, 'I'm an Alsatian'. Of course, he was on his back, and my mouth was on his throat at the time. After that incident, we became good friends. I guess you could call him my best friend. Sorry Hoomans, you just got fired.

CHAPTER 5

Back to our story. I told Bhilla what's up and put him on the trail of Chandu. Bhilla is exactly half my size and, in Hooman terms, if I'm John Abraham, he's Cyrus Broacha. (Please don't ask me who that is, the publisher has forced me to use the reference.) Bhilla slipped away from Sea View to out of view, just like Chandu. Now, I had no option but to sit around outside this horrendous, unhygienic, uncared for and unloved building that was erroneously named till Bhilla returned. Oh, and when he did return, what a tale he had to tell.

Bhilla talks very fast, so if I write down everything he said, I'd fill three more books. Plus Hoomans don't speak Dogolease. Did I mention before that Hoomans believe that they are the most advanced species? Here's what Bhilla had to say as translated and summarized from the original Dogolease. Please don't be critical of spelling mistakes. 'King Franco, he was standing near the lift, smelling as bad as this building, and talking on his mobile phone very animatedly. Luckily, I speak and comprehend all Hooman languages. He was talking to a guy called Ranjan, who seemed like his boss. I figured this out because Chandu kept referring to Ranjan as Boss. King Franco. They did it. Or at least they are part of the gang that's involved in Hakuna Matata's dognapping. Chandu kept reassuring Ranjan that no one had a clue about the whole incident. He said he spoke to very prominent people like Smellji. Chandu called him the most prominent member of the entire area, as he's the only watchman, not to have been fired in the last three years. Ranjan then told Chandu to call Chikoo, and update him. Chandu went up in the lift, and I think he works on the second floor!'

I thanked Bhilla for a job well done. Now we were getting somewhere. However, now we needed to get somewhere else, cause our super-sensitive dog noses couldn't bear the stench of Sea View. Wish they called it Sea Smells, for Dog's sake! Once back in our lane, I told Bhilla, we needed to hatch a plan to get to that phone. The next piece of the puzzle was 'Chikoo', and the route was through Chandu's mobile phone. Hakuna Matata, we are coming. Or, we will be coming, as the day was almost done. The sun was starting to set, so I needed to get back before Homi and Dirty Perry started fighting over who lost me. Can someone PLEASE tell me how Hoomans are the most intelligent species on Earth? PLEASE!

I woke up the following morning to find that it was a

Sunday. Hoomans never cease to surprise me. You guys have so many ridiculous customs and traditions. For example, you have school holidays in the summer instead of the monsoon. If dogs ran Hooman society (and one day we will), we'd definitely have a monsoon break instead. Dogs and Hoomans both don't like the rain, and it's a much bigger menace than the sun. Close the country down in the monsoon, I say.

Then this concept of a rest day. This Sunday thingee. Today's Hoomans hardly move on any day of the week. They get transported in machines, then sit at desks, occasionally walking to toilets. Who needs rest from that? And that too an entire day? Rest from sitting in a vehicle. Rest from sitting at a desk. Rest from the digital pressure to send inane useless messages. So, this whole Sunday off concept seems pointless to me. I can't even say the word Sunday with a straight face (of course, there is a small matter of Alsatians, all having beautiful, triangular, faces).

Contrast this behaviour with us canines. Monday to Sunday, we follow the same schedule. Get up, go for a walk, pee, poop, come home, eat. Again get up, go for a walk, pee and maybe poop. We just rinse and repeat, four or five times a day, every day. No breaks, no rest, no Sunday off. Sunday, what a load of total nonsense. Even by ridiculous Hooman standards.

CHAPTER 6

For the sake of the reader, not giving up reading all together, I'll proceed with my story. Okay, 'my' story sounds like it's all fabricated. Like I said before, there is some truth. A little, less than a little, but some truth, I think.

It being Sunday, in many ways it was the worst day to conduct an investigation as all Hoomans would be in their homes. How, in that case, would we be able to procure (I feel that's a much classier word than steal) Chandu's phone? After I dropped Homi back home from his morning walk, I howled up our vice-captain, Mr Bhilla. We met outside my building and hatched a plan. Chandu worked on the second floor. But he would have to come down to smoke his beedi. We decided, and by we, I mean just me, that Bhilla would wait outside Sea View for him, then signal to me so I could join him and then we'd enact the second part of our ingenious plot. I returned home, had

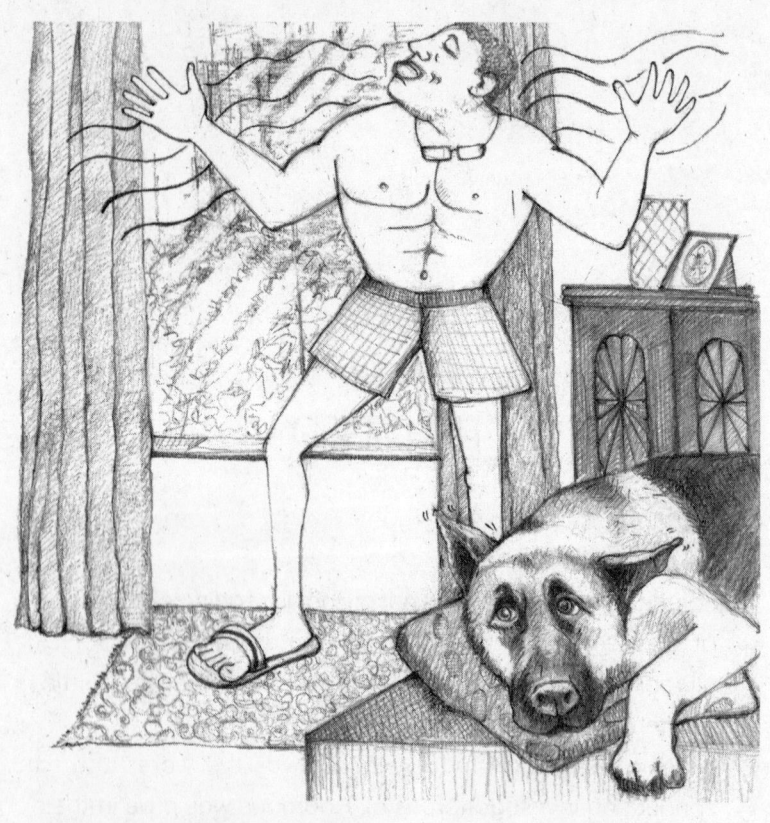

my breakfast, then had Homi's breakfast, and took a nap, as per my normal routine. Soon, I was rudely awakened to Homi singing his favourite Opera 'Cosi Fan Tute'. Opera's great, and I like Mozart myself, but Homi's rendition was so bad that the only thought a bystander would have is that of wishing that they'd never been born. Yet, the powerful canine ear picked up Bhilla's call to arms over the horrid singing. Homi, meanwhile, tried to catch the note, the powerful high, and failed completely and put out his back with the strain. He started screaming in pain, writhing on the floor, calling out to Dirty Perry for help. She in turn was doing her manicure, pedicure, and screamed back at Homi, mentioning in between the profanity that it was not the right time. He, poor fellow, was waiting on the floor, explaining that no one can choose when their back goes out. In all that cacophony, I found my chance to escape unnoticed.

Within fourteen seconds, I reached the lane that led to Sea View. Bhilla was super excited. So excited that he had to execute a wee pee. 'He's there,' Bhilla pointed out. Sure enough, Chandu was standing outside the building gate, mobile phone in his left hand, beedi in his right. Bhilla and I exchanged looks. We knew at that exact moment, we had less than a minute to execute part two of our cunning plan, which was to remove the mobile phone from Chandu's hand, if possible, without his knowledge. It was time to pull out the full bag of doggie tricks.

Hoomans, let me introduce you to a trick called 'The Imaginary Cat'. This is a hand-me-down from several generations of Alsatians. As you know, Hoomans can be very mean and cruel towards doggies. It's difficult for us doggies to fight back. This is because Hoomans control the police, the municipality, the courts, the parliament, even the building security. This is why I burst out laughing whenever one Hooman asks another Hooman, 'Does your dog bite?' It's us dogs who need to ask you Hoomans the

question, not the other way around. Now, many years ago, somewhere in Germany, a really smart dog came up with a trick to hit back at his tormentors. These was a group of three teenage boys who liked to throw stones at passing dogs. Finally, having had enough, this one smart canine came up with a brand-new hustle. The three villains were leaning against a car. The dog pretended that there was a cat under the car, and made a quick charge, reaching under the side of the car by going between the legs of these monsters. All three terror suspects got the fright of their life, and fell to the floor in a very undignified fashion. All the dogs in the locality fell too, but they fell with laughter. There is also a date to prove the sport of rugby was born from this incident. Some smart sports scientist replaced the imaginary cat with the ball, and the car with a field a few years later. Of course, the main part of the trick is to continue and follow through with the action, chasing after the imaginary cat across the road ahead. This gives the event the status of an 'accident'. So, human retaliation becomes unlikely. Great invention. Second only to air-conditioning and ice-cream in my humble opinion. Poor Chandu was going to be the unsuspecting target of 'The Imaginary Cat'.

Oh how he screamed like a little baby! Tell me, Hoomans, why do you use phrases like, 'ran like a cur' or 'died a dog's death'? Horrible and untrue. In truth, it's you Hoomans who squeal and run like ... well, er, Hoomans, because no animal is as cowardly, really. Look at Chandu. He was so startled by my tackle to his knees, that he leapt in the air, making unnatural sounds. I do believe that the sounds came from all sorts of places, not just his mouth. Obviously the mobile and beedi flew out of his hands, and Bhilla, in one swoop, retrieved the phone, and unnecessarily the beedi. Even as Chandu's feet and body fell to the floor, Bhilla and I had vanished. Here I put forth a request for a new phrase to be used: 'as swift as a dog'. All those in favour please send the publisher an e-mail, thanking you in advance.

But now I had a bit of a problem. Hoomans' mobile phones are not easy to access for us doggies. Our paws are flatter and more rotund. We don't have delicate fragile little fingers that will allow us to press a digit as small as an eyelash. You really need to involve us animals in science and technology. Most of your gadgets are very anti-animal in design. It's tough to hold a mobile phone for us doggies anyway, as we prefer using our mouths for carrying things and our hands for walking. The metal surface makes it a painful carry and the design is so dog unfriendly that it's brutally impossible to take selfies. Real drag. Yet, if we wanted to crack open the case of Hakuna Matata, we needed to access the contents of the phone. Unlike Hoomans, we have so many varieties of canines, that obviously one would have digits mirroring hideous Hooman fingers. Luckily for me and Bhilla, we knew one such canine specimen. Her name was Mrs Peepu, and she had the longest fingers, which is very common for her tribe, the Dachshunds. I hope you Hoomans have been paying attention. I'm working really hard here putting together this story for you.

Mrs Peepu lived in a building near mine. Since today was a Sunday, she would probably come down for her walk at 3.30pm which was a few hours away. But we got lucky. She suddenly appeared outside her building in her car. It turns out that she had gone to visit a family nearby, and typical Hoomans decided to use the car for this distance of 200 meters. Mrs Peepu jumped out of the vehicle and responded to our calls. Just like me, she has disciplined the Sharma family that she adopted. While Mother Sharma waited for her, we took Mrs Peepu aside and mouthed over the phone. (How can I say handed, when it goes from the mouth directly, na?) Mrs Peepu, who has a massive crush on me (who wouldn't?), used her fine scarcely used nails to open the phone. We quickly went into Chandu's WhatsApp. We noticed that he couldn't spell a single word

correctly. The auto-correct setting had been thoroughly defeated and destroyed. The messages with Ranjan were very short, so Bhilla had an idea. We memorized Ranjan and Chikoo's phone numbers. Then we thanked Mrs Peepu for her service, I think she tried to kiss me, but she's only five inches off the ground, and her surge upwards towards me only reached my right forearm. I stopped Bhilla from laughing and we took off, before Mrs Peepu could lunge again.

CHAPTER 7

We returned to Chandu's unkempt abode. The poor idiot was searching under every car parked outside the building. In fact, we found him face down under a grey SUV, only his knees and feet visible. Bhilla placed the phone and beedi between his legs. One minute later, we heard a squeal of delight. The idiot that he is, he thought he had found the missing phone himself. What's that word Homi uses for Dirty Perry, when he's sure she can't hear him? Ah that's right. 'Moron.' Moron would be apt for Chandu.

Bhilla and I knew what to do next. We needed to locate addresses from the phone numbers. For that we needed the help of an Alsatian cousin of mine, Rocky. Rocky is a police dog, attached to the nearby police station. However, first I had to check all was fine at home. It had been a while and I didn't want Dirty Perry to start nagging Homi.

I mean that would happen anyway. But not because of me, hopefully. I told Bhilla to wait in the lane and that I'd return in, as you Hoomans call it, 'a jiffy'. Why do you call it 'a jiffy'? The word makes no sense. It has no genesis, no backstory evolution. We doggies don't have any senseless words. You can trace all our words to their origin. Each and every one makes perfect sense, With a backstory, history and evolution. Hoomans! Who designated you as the advanced species, who? For dog's sake, WHO???

Back home, I quickly organized an early lunch for myself. Put your hands down, I hear you, I get your question, please stop yelling, 'How did I organize my early lunch'? Very simple answer. Roxy, of course. In every dog family, there's at least one member who feels guilty that they don't do enough for the dog of the house. In the Treasurywalla family, that would be Roxy. Her mind was basically on boys, and fashion, and boys, and trends, and boys, and pop culture, and boys, and her friends and boys. Did I mention boys? She knew that Homi was doing all the hard yards with a little help from Dirty Perry. Hoomans, for the record, patting your doggie twice a day does not constitute looking after. With Roxy, all I had to do was go to the fridge and whine a little. Overcome by guilt, she immediately took out my food, and fed me. The food was the usual chicken stock with rice, and a soupy gravy, with a few diced veggies thrown in. The veggies, I consistently ignore. Yet, they consistently and incessantly put them in my food. It's so hard to train dull-witted Hoomans.

Meal done, I left for work. Come on peeps. You know I had a job to do. Thanks Roxy. Bhilla, the sweet lieutenant, was exactly where I had left him. I carried a few biscuits in my mouth for him, as it's still too complicated to get Roxy to understand the doggie bag concept. The police station was about seven minutes away. Seven minutes for us doggies is about twenty-two minutes for Hoomans. And for the real unfit ones it's closer to thirty minutes. This is why doggies, you must get your Hoomans to jog when you are walking alongside them.

Rocky is almost all black and likes to sit at the top of the steps at the entrance to the station. This position deters the half-hearted complainant from actually entering. You know the type, with the complaints like:

(a) My top floor neighbours are playing the drums too loudly.

(b) My watchman doesn't open the gate for me.

(c) Every time my wife leaves the home, she comes back.

Yup, these are real complaints. We pulled Rocky to the side and gave him the scoop, after which he was super eager to be involved. He mentioned only two things, 'Hakuna Matata', what a peculiar name?' Then he added, 'But why hasn't the Subramanian family made a complaint by now, especially if a day has passed? Very strange'. I looked at Bhilla. Bhilla looked at me. Clearly, we had no answers. Time for Rocky to do his thing and get us the possible villains of this entire episode, Ranjan and Chikoo.

Don't ask me how he did it. I told you this book will have plenty of holes in it. Suffice to say that most of us dogs won't seem obvious to an innocent, unknowing bystander. Rocky took the phone in and, ten minutes later, he brought it back. He had managed to find out and memorize both the addresses. Problem was, Chikoo's address was in Jamshedpur, Jharkhand, millions of miles away. This meant that Ranjan now was the key. We had to find him and hopefully, his trail would lead to Chikoo. (For anyone who has started reading the book from here, let me clarify that Chikoo appears to be a man, and not a fruit, although occasionally one could be mistaken for the other.) Inspector Rocky then said that he'd join us in the chase. Thus, it became official police business. The only problem was that three dogs together would be conspicuous. Ranjan may thus get a warning before time. So instead, we followed each other at two-minute intervals. Remember, we just needed to follow each other's scent, which as you know is the doggie GPS. It was decided that Bhilla, the best nose and tracker out of the three of us, would take the lead. Ranjan's address? Forty-one minutes away at a brisk pace for me. Two hours sixteen minutes for Hoomans on foot. Thank God, we did not have any Hoomans to slow us down. Let the chase begin.

CHAPTER 8

Ranjan's house is in what Hoomans call a chawl. It's not quite a fancy place, nor is it quite a decrepit place. The problem with chawls is that more and more chawlwallas have dogs these days. In fact, there are doggies everywhere. The moment we reached nearby, let's say 500 yards from Ranjan's address, the dog symphony started. The big difference between dog politics and Hooman politics is that Hoomans lie and go back on their word routinely. We doggies are not so comfortable with lies, and just manage a basic understanding of deceit. I counted seventeen distinct barks. Just to share with you the kind of questions these barks were asking:

1. Who are you?

2. Did you bring food?

3. Biscuits? Please say you got biscuits.

4. Do you want to fight?

5. Let's all chase the cats?

6. In the movie 'Baby', what was the dog actor's real name?

The problem was that the racket would alert Ranjan. I had to come up with a plan superfast. First, we needed to move the acoustics away from Ranjan. So Rocky and I took off in the opposite direction leaving Bhilla to play scout and try gaining access (once there was relative silence) into Ranjan's house. We moved west off Ranjan's house. For Hoomans, that would be east. For you Hoomans, you look at geography while facing. We measure it while facing away. This is why animals can escape storms, while Hoomans often run headfirst into them. The barking orchestra followed Rocky and me. The questions changed:

1. Where are you going?

2. Let me sniff your behind first, na?

3. Have you brought food or not?

4. Do you like balls?

5. Wait for me, please?

Rocky and I felt it was mainly inquisitiveness. Once we were far enough, sound-wise, from Ranjan's, we decided to engage with the Chawl 17. This could be dangerous because like I've told you Hoomans 100 times, dogs are more straightforward, so a confrontation like this is straight fight or flight, or paw shake. Although sometimes, we land up doing all three in the span of three minutes.

The seventeen desi dogs formed three distinct groups. Even though we were outnumbered, we were Alsatians. All doggies know of famous doggie folklore, or dog lore, as we like to call it. Dog lore is replete with stories of Alsatians taking on and defeating as many as nine Hooman criminals at a time. There is one magnificent story of how an Alsatian lured an angry elephant away from Hoomans and back into the forest. Our reputation preceded us. A brown dog, almost our size, came forward with slightly bared fangs. He came close enough, so I had to bare mine. At that point, one female doggie from the middle group said, 'Wait, that's my boyfriend Rocky'. We found out later Rocky had dated

Lina, a couple of seasons ago, although they had not kept in touch. What can I tell you? Everyone loves us Alsatians. We're so ruggedly handsome, it's hard to be humble. As for Rocky, he's known to be quite the 'dog', if you know what I mean. (The publisher has requested me not to elaborate on these things, as our expected Hooman readership has plunged under 1½ years of age).

CHAPTER 9

Soon we got good news, and even 'gooder' news. Led by Lina, the dog pack decided to help us. The 'gooder' news? Not a single dog had a kind woof to say about Ranjan. Let me elaborate, dear Hooman, as you just don't understand Dogychology (Dog Psychology). Doggies basically divide Hoomankind into three types:

Type 1. Love doggies. Are kind and affectionate. Sometimes too affectionate. Case in point, Dirty Perry.

Type 2. People who are indifferent to doggies. Not interested in them, but not mean or wicked. This is the largest group, they just would neither pet, nor throw a stone at a dog. The reasons for this are many, like no dogs in their childhood for exposure, or the fact that they are extremely, morbidly lazy and lastly that there are no stones available in their vicinity.

Type 3. The third group is the vicious Hooman category. The ones who have no empathy for dogs. Always want to get rid of us. Throw things, shout abuses and are empty, soulless, malicious malcontents, and a complete disgrace to all living organisms.

Ranjan fell in this category, so the seventeen local canines had a distinct dislike of him. This was all very well, but we needed a plan. Remember Ranjan had the connection to Chikoo. Chikoo was the next piece in the puzzle. Bhilla had been fantastic. He checked the house using doggie x-ray vision. I suppose, you'll need an explanation for that. Really, writing this book for Hoomans is like teaching a baby how to eat. A dog's nose is actually better than x-ray vision glasses. X-ray vision allows you to see through things, mostly from a close distance. This pales in comparison to the power and facilities of a canine nose. Let me give you an example. When Hoomans travel, they pass through security checks at airports, where the machine can see what's in your bag and clothes. Our noses let us do that and more. We can smell and read a Hooman's soul, their intent, their thoughts, their moods, all from analyzing their normally foul aromas. Hoomans, of course, can't smell how bad they actually smell. This is because of far inferior noses. Not only do they have poor nasal potential, but 50% of Hoomans have colds. This makes the poor nasal power even more inadequate.

Bhilla did a comprehensive examination of Ranjan's position. This answered the important questions:

1. Ranjan was at home.

2. He was sleeping on his back, with his mouth wide open.

3. He was horrible to look at.

4. He was alone, and his phone was on the floor near his outstretched hand.

Since there were twenty of us, we needed a small precision style striking squad of maybe four individuals to infiltrate and carry out the operation, in what would be about seven Hooman seconds. Bear in mind, four dogs to go in and out with phone in mouth in that much time. It was decided (and by that I mean I decided) that Rocky, me and two of the fastest canines would form this group. Lina suggested Chotu and Tommy. Chotu was really tiny. Tommy was the fastest dog in the area, by a mile. He had that high waist and strong hind quarters to prove it. Definitely part Saluki. Oh, Hoomans, please stop spreading rubbish about the greyhounds being the fastest dogs. Let me educate you that after about 800 metres, the Saluki is the fastest, and please don't argue, you are the same idiots who make doggies wear shoes.

CHAPTER 10

Back to operation Ranjan. It was still daylight, so we had to be completely inconspicuous. The plan was simple. Tommy pushes Chotu through a tiny window. Chotu then needs to open the bigger window below it for three of us to enter separately, a few seconds apart. Bhilla would stand guard outside. Lina and the others would start a mock dog fight to cause a diversion in case Ranjan woke up.

Once inside, we were shocked at the living conditions. For me, especially, it was a real smack to the system. Thanks to Dirty Perry and Roxy, I was used to clean carpets and upholstered furniture, all ornaments and accessories in an organized setting. Above all, the Treasurywallas were big on hygiene. Ranjan had obviously never heard of the word hygiene. As for orderly and stylish, I don't think he

was familiar with those terms either. Rocky got distracted for a second upon seeing some 'chura' and rancid wafers strewn on the floor. There was the foul stench of the liquid that Hoomans often like to drink lying about in an open bottle. Papers and clips were littered everywhere, and so were banned plastic bags. Rocky observed that if we didn't get him on kidnapping, we could most definitely charge him with environmental degradation.

The bad smell from his breath meant that he was in a deep stupor. His phone was still on some music channel, the sound of the beats and his snoring giving us a sound cushion. Suddenly, he moved his hand to pick up the phone, then even as he grasped it, he fell back to sleep. The snoring continued. The same irritating song on a loop was so annoying, I needed to end the operation just so that I could get away from the horrible tune and Ranjan as soon as possible.

Chotu now had the delicate job of the removing the phone from Ranjan's right hand. He tried, but the Hooman's grip was firm. Too firm for a drunk, unconscious man, but we had no time to figure that out. We just needed the phone. Rocky then came up with an old police dog trick. Hoomans have super sensitive ears. He sent some Alsatian breath into Ranjan's right ear. It worked. And it didn't work. Without waking Ranjan, Rocky slapped his ears with his free hand. So, we moved it up a notch. Rocky and I both sent hot breath into his ears simultaneously. Ranjan dropped the phone, and dug both his ears with his hands, luckily without waking up. Chotu grabbed the phone. Tommy grabbed Chotu, and both cleared the window in one move. Rocky, however, stopped. He wanted to examine the room for any other evidence, since our target was out cold. Eventually, Rocky failed. Hoomans, please, please, understand that if you provide odious smells, it's a hundred times worse on a dog's olfactory machine. Ranjan's room odour defeated all of us; we had to bid a silent retreat. In sports terms, let's call that a draw.

Within seconds, we had a new problem. Rocky, the professional that he is, quickly went through the phone like a dog on a bone. Which, by the way, rhymes, 'Like a Dog on a Bone, like a Dog on a Phone'. Strangely, no mention of Chikoo in the address list. No messages, no WhatsApp, nothing. This meant one of two things. Did Ranjan have a second phone? Or were messages to Chikoo going the old-fashioned way? We did a doggie huddle. All twenty of us. We used the many minds are better than one theory. (In doggie speak, that's many tails are better than one.) I explained the dead end we were in, but as soon as I mentioned Chikoo, Lina started jumping up and down in a straight line. Hoomans may recall that some dogs have this knack of jumping up and down and landing exactly on the same spot. When it happens, it seems unreal, like a compilation of highlights of the exact same thing. Once she calmed down, Lina spoke excitedly. 'Chikoo? Chikoo, he lives just outside this colony. He's a gardener. But he's a dog lover, feeds us dogs all the time, he can't be involved, he's super nice.' Oh Dog, here we go again. Now I was really feeling like I was going to be defeated. That is, if I was a Labrador. However, Alsatians are dogs of steel.

A general discussion ensued. Most of the pack knew of Chikoo, and all agreed with Lina. In the meantime, Chotu and Rocky reentered Ranjan's room, dropped off the phone, did an insincere search for four-and-a-half seconds, and then rushed out, meaning that they couldn't breathe. Keep in mind that dogs can't really hold their noses tight like Hoomans. To rid us off distasteful smells, we basically smell each other as quickly as possible, till the old stench has left our systems.

Forget the second phone, we had a hot clue. There was a Chikoo, we knew where he lived, and he was possibly the last piece of the puzzle. Only one thing did not make sense. If he was a real authentic genuine dog lover, how and why would he have any involvement in Hakuna Matata's kidnapping? However, it was going to be dark soon. As both de facto and de jure leader, I made my decision. Lina, Rocky, Bhilla and myself would head off to Chikoo's residence. Lina assured us that there was no need for backup. I tried to argue, but she wouldn't stop jumping up and down. So, I stopped, so that she would stop too. I could feel another huge surge of adrenaline. My ASP (Alsatian Sensory Perception), told me this was the final clue to the caper. In ten minutes, we reached a ramshackle little shanty, with a blue plastic tarpaulin making for a makeshift roof. The house, (I'm generously going to call it a house) stood alone. Almost like it was being punished by society. (I'm generously going to use the word society). This time though, Lina led the way.

A really short bespectacled man with large eyes, that made him look like an owl came out. We were all taken aback at his reaction. He squealed with delight. Pure joy. This is a common occurrence among Hoomans that love dogs. Like Dirty Perry for instance. They all get extremely vocal with joy. Also, you may notice their speech impediments while talking to the dog, whose very presence brings them unbridled joy. They start speaking like infant Hoomans and make up ridiculous words. These words are more sounds than actual words. For example, 'Who is this coochy poochy poopoo?' Then there is, 'Look at this Gingamaa Leeleelorpaga?' Just sounds associated with the onset of madness and delirium. Remember, though, as dogs in a Hooman world, we just have to take our victories wherever they come. Recent research shows there are more Hoomans who don't like dogs, than Hoomans who do. (This research was conducted by an entirely canine division, consisting of nine doggie scientists led by the famous, senior analyst, a Siberian Husky called Fred (Professor Fred Fuigus, full name). The owl, meanwhile, rushed to pet Lina, then the rest of us. His tone changed to the sweet nothing sounds and expressions I've mentioned above. I was astounded. I'll tell you why? I mean, I better tell you why. Otherwise, how

do either of us proceed with this story, na?

As Chikoo the owl patted me, my ASP gave its usual thorough character report. It said that Chikoo was genuine. A genuine, kind, affectionate, altruistic, dog lover. My ASP can never be wrong. It's not a faulty machine built by Hoomans. It is a work of art perfected in our DNA over hundreds of years! I was really bewildered. I checked with Rocky, Bhilla and Lina, who all confirmed my report, equally puzzled. If the owl was not the villain, what the hell was going on? Chikoo went inside his hutment and emerged with a packet of Marie biscuits. I had two problems with this. Firstly, biscuits are by and large not good for our digestive systems. Secondly, as a member of the upwardly mobile, affluent dog community, I was used to treats like liver paté and mutton cutlets (and also the cutlets with beard known as Dareewalla Cutlet). Yet, we all ate the biscuits. I mean, we couldn't give anything away. The idea was to lull the owl into trusting us implicitly, which seemed to be where our relationship was headed. Dog lover or not, he had to know what was going on.

I took Lina aside and told her and Bhilla to keep Chikoo occupied. We needed a quick check of the quarters. Bhilla pretended to have something stuck in his paw. The good-natured owl immediately responded by doing a thorough check of all four paws. Yes, yes, I know, it was a bit devious. But remember, who taught doggies to be a little devious? Who? Hoomans is the right answer. While Chikoo was busy checking Bhilla's paws, we got just enough time to get into the ramshackle tin can house. Here, we found a bed, a small chest with clothes, a pot of water and a table fan. That was it. We were about to leave when we heard it.

A small sound. Rocky thought it was the door, but then we all picked up a scent. A very clear scent. A very familiar scent. We all froze except for Lina. Lina was swift, rushing to the source of both sound and scent. It was under that little bed of Chikoo's. While Lina struggled to get below the low bed, Bhilla caught on to the scent and moved like lightning. He was in, he was under, and he was out. Filled to the brim with excitement, he exclaimed, 'Doggies, you just won't believe it.' We all looked at him, urging him on. Rocky even tried growling in an effort to intimidate Bhilla into speaking faster. However, as it turned out, there was no way to speak as the answer emerged from under the bed. Looking quite good for what he may have gone through, it was the dog named after the phrase himself, Hakuna Matata!

CHAPTER 11

Hoomans think that dogs can't express surprise. That really surprises me. Now, of all the available expressions, surprise is the loudest one for canines to exhibit. We Alsatians are the kings of the surprised look. We wrinkle and furrow our brows, turn our handsome heads to the side, and open our mouths, tongue hanging out. If that doesn't spell surprised, I'll be even more surprised. You can guess by now that Rocky and I looked like what you Hoomans would call a boy band photograph. Same clothes, same look, same posture. The first thing I observed was that Bhilla and Hakuna Matata were the same size. The second, more surprising observation was that the Affenpinscher seemed quite happy. You'd expect a kidnapped dog to be a little bedraggled, worn out, anxious or at least tired. Hakuna Matata was just happy and, if anything, a little unbothered about everything. I call it the 'short dog complex'. It's when tiny dogs compensate for their 'smallness' by being extra cocky, even standoffish in their posture and manner. Hakuna Matata just looked around, took in the scene, then as if he was bored stiff, he calmly went back under the bed, as if to say, 'This is clearly a waste of my time'. Bhilla rushed out to inform Lina and the others.

With all our barking and excited body language, Chikoo came running in. From our faces, he knew that we knew. And since we knew, he knew that there was some explaining to do. Lucky for us, Hooman dog lovers love talking aloud to us dogs. I'm not just saying that to find closure to the story. This is an absolute fact. Oh, and also, I need to find closure to this story. Looking a little guilty, Chikoo sat down, and started his apologination. (That's the combination of an apology and an explanation. Never fear language, Hoomans. Language should fear you.)

'Someone contacted Chandu to take away Hakuna Matata, but wanted Hakunajee to get a nice home. So Chandu, the borderline criminal, reached out to Ranjan, the career criminal, who contacted me, cause they both know I love dogs. I know I don't have money, but Hakunajee is quite happy here,' Chikoo said remorsefully. Then came the crusher as he added, 'Do you know who organized all this? It was Mr. Subramanian himself.' Once again, we put on our surprise mask. Two complete surprises in just two Hooman minutes. Unbelievable.

Chikoo went on to explain how Mr Subramanian was jealous of all the attention Mrs Subramanian was giving Hakuna Matata. Mr Subramanian never really liked dogs. Or any animals. Or people. Or himself. But, he did like Mrs Subramanian, and wanted her to like him, at least occasionally. Chikoo was feeling very bad. However, Rocky and I desired a happy ending for all. We took Hakuna Matata back, and just pretended that he had wandered and got lost. Mrs Subramanian was so thrilled, she leapt in the air, which scared the living daylights out of Hakuna Matata. Let's just say Mrs Subramanian was not the most athletic figure in the neighbourhood. Hakuna Matata tried his best to continue signalling his indifference to everything.

Now let's come to Mr Subramanian. He was one of those skinny fat Hoomans. Skinny everywhere, but with a big paunch where perhaps some nutrition was stored for a rainy day. His surprise at seeing Hakuna Matata would put an Alsatian to shame. He gingerly patted Hakuna Matata with tears in his eyes. Both Subramanians had tears in their eyes, but for very different reasons. When we found the appropriate moment, Rocky and I had a casual word with Mr Subramanian. Oh, and by word, I mean one long look. A look which said, 'We know, you know, we know what you did. Make sure this never happens again.' Mr Subramanian grinned sheepishly and nodded in agreement. Hakuna Matata had already fallen asleep in Mrs Subramanian's lap. The fact of the matter is that on average anyone will fall asleep within two complete sentences uttered by Mrs Subramanian. Rocky had already started to yawn.

We left the premises; our work here was done. Another crime caper solved by Franco and friends. (It was my first time, but 'another' sounds way cooler). I felt immense

satisfaction, and I realized that I had found my true calling, in the pawsteps of Rocky's famous grandfather 'Ranjha'. A true-blue dog detective. I couldn't wait to share this news with Homi, Roxy and Dirty Perry. They would be so proud. But then again, I don't think they would let me out if they found out about my new vocation. So, let's just keep this between ourselves.

ACKNOWLEDGEMENTS

To my father, Farrokh, my mother, Olivia, my wife, Ayesha, and my children Mikhaail and Maya, we may disagree about many things, but definitely agree on one, 'Dogs First, last and forever'.

And above all to all you beautiful doggies, rich and poor, breeds and strays, thank you for everything. Oh, and if there are no dogs in heaven, send me straight to hell.

ABOUT THE AUTHOR

Cyrus Broacha is an out of work actor, singer, dancer, writer, weight-lifter and above all dog lover. His success can be deemed from the fact that at 53, he still has not moved out of his mother's house, and is continually borrowing money and clothes from his good friend Kunal Vijayakar. Cyrus, for sure has only one redeeming quality, he lives his life with the only honest truth he knows, which is,
"Dogs Before Men".

ABOUT THE ILLUSTRATOR

Ayesha Broacha is a photographer and illustrator, mother to two grown kids, an amateur tri athlete . . . and the ever patient and loving wife to the author. I can't sing or write . . . but I can draw!

ACKNOWLEDGEMENTS

To my father, Farrokh, my mother, Olivia, my wife, Ayesha, and my children Mikhaail and Maya, we may disagree about many things, but definitely agree on one, 'Dogs First, last and forever'.

And above all to all you beautiful doggies, rich and poor, breeds and strays, thank you for everything. Oh, and if there are no dogs in heaven, send me straight to hell.

ABOUT THE AUTHOR

Cyrus Broacha is an out of work actor, singer, dancer, writer, weight-lifter and above all dog lover. His success can be deemed from the fact that at 53, he still has not moved out of his mother's house, and is continually borrowing money and clothes from his good friend Kunal Vijayakar. Cyrus, for sure has only one redeeming quality, he lives his life with the only honest truth he knows, which is,
"Dogs Before Men".

ABOUT THE ILLUSTRATOR

Ayesha Broacha is a photographer and illustrator, mother to two grown kids, an amateur tri athlete . . . and the ever patient and loving wife to the author. I can't sing or write . . . but I can draw!